Lights! Camera! Wubbzy!

NICK JR. WOW! WOW! WUBBZY!

Adapted by
Lauren Cecil

SCHOLASTIC INC.
New York   Toronto   London   Auckland
Sydney   Mexico City   New Delhi   Hong Kong

ISBN-13: 978-0-545-19723-6
ISBN-10: 0-545-19723-6
Based on the TV series *Wow! Wow! Wubbzy!* as seen on Nick Jr.® created by Bob Boyle.
© 2009 Bolder Media, Inc. and Starz Media, LLC. All rights reserved.
Wow! Wow! Wubbzy! and all related titles, logos, and characters are trademarks of Bolder Media, Inc./Starz Media, LLC.
www.wubbzy.com
Published by Scholastic Inc. SCHOLASTIC and associated logos are trademarks and/or registered trademarks of Scholastic Inc.

12 11 10 9 8 7 6 5 4 3 2 1   9 10 11 12 13 14/0
Printed in the U.S.A.
First printing, August 2009

Wubbzy was in Wuzzlewood to sing with the Wubb Girlz. They were the most popular singing group in the whole world!

"Wubbzy, are you excited to sing in front of millions of people tonight?" the reporter Jann Starl asked.

All of a sudden, Wubbzy felt very nervous. "M-m-millions of p-p-people?" he stammered.

Wubbzy headed to the dressing room where he ran into the Wubb Girlz—Shine, Shimmer, and Sparkle.

"Hi, Wubbzy!" Shine called. "Are you ready to put on a great show for all our fans?"

"Well . . . I g-g-guess," Wubbzy said.

Wubbzy went to practice. Denever the opera singer
mouth, all that came out was a hould get hypnotized.
"Oh no!" gasped Wubbzy. "I car
going to do?"

"Just keep your eyes on the watch," Walden instructed.
"You're getting sleepy. . . ." he said slowly as he swung the
watch back and forth. "You're a great singer . . . you love
to sing . . . you can't wait to sing onstage. . . ."

Suddenly, Walden became stiff and his eyes glazed over. "I'm a great singer!" he shouted. He sang in a loud operatic voice, "Mi-mi-mi-mi!" "Uh-oh! I think Walden just hypnotized himself!" said Wubbzy.

"I wonder if it worked on me, too!" said Wubbzy. He opened his mouth to sing. *Squeak!*

"It's no use. I can't do it!" Wubbzy moaned.

"Maybe a new outfit will help!" Daizy suggested.

She took Wubbzy to the wardrobe room. He tried on lots of different outfits, but none of them was quite right.

Just then, Widget arrived with Walden. "Well, the good news is that Walden doesn't think he's an opera singer anymore," Widget announced. "But the bad news is that now he thinks he's a monkey."

"At least he stopped singing!" sighed Daizy.

"And so have I!" Wubbzy groaned.

"Don't worry, Wubbster," said Widget. "I can fix this!"

"Ta da!" Widget cried as she unveiled her invention.
"It's the Wow Wow 3000!"
"Wow, wow!" Wubbzy exclaimed. "It looks just like me!"
"And it sings like you, too!" explained Widget.

"See, Wubbzy," began Widget, "the Wow Wow 3000 can sing and dance onstage for you."

"Wow, Widget, this is great!" gushed Wubbzy. "Uh-oh! Here come the Wubb Girlz! I'd better hide!"

"Hey, Wubbzy," Shine said to the robot. "Are you ready?"
"Wow, wow, wow! Let's go!" cheered the robot.
"All right!" sang Shimmer, Sparkle, and Shine.

The Wubb Girlz and the Wow Wow 3000 were waiting to go onstage.
"Wow wow wow! Wow wow wow!" sang the Wow Wow 3000.
"Not yet, Wubbzy," hushed Shine, "the song hasn't even started!"
"WOW WOW WOW! WOW WOW WOW!" The robot sang louder.

"Wubbzy, sshhh!" said Shine.

"WOWWOWWOW WOWWOWWOW!" the robot yelled.

Then—POW!—the Wow Wow 3000 exploded!

"What?!?" gasped Shine. "Wubbzy is a ROBOT?!"

Wubbzy poked his head out of his hiding spot.
"What's going on?" Shine asked the real Wubbzy.
"I'm sorry for tricking you," said Wubbzy. "I was too nervous to sing, so Widget made a robot that would sing for me."

"The Wubb Girlz know about stage fright, too!" Shine said.

"You do?" asked Wubbzy.

"Of course! But performing for a big crowd isn't as scary when the three of us are together!" she explained. "Maybe if you brought your friends with you onstage, you wouldn't feel so nervous!"

"Good idea!" Wubbzy exclaimed.

"Ladies and gentlemen," said an announcer, "put your hands together for the Wubb Girlz—with very special guests, Wubbzy . . . and friends!"

"*Ooooooh! Sing a song! Sing, sing, sing along!*"
Shimmer, Shine, and Sparkle sang.
"*Wow! Wow!*" Wubbzy and his friends joined in.

The crowd was still going wild as the gang headed offstage.
"Wubbzy, what a show!" Jann Starl said.
"I couldn't have done it without my friends!" said Wubbzy.

"You guys did a great job, too!" the reporter said to Widget, Walden, and Daizy. "Do you have anything to say to the millions of people watching on television?"

"M-m-millions of p-p-people?" stuttered Daizy.

"T-t-t-television?" stammered Widget.

"*Oooh! Oooh! Oooh!*" Walden grunted like a monkey.

"Wow, wow!" Wubbzy laughed. "Looks like I'm not the only one with stage fright!"